**FRANKIE'S
MAGIC
FOOTBALL**

BY FRANK LAMPARD

FRANKIE VS THE COWBOY'S CREW
FRANK LAMPARD

LITTLE, BROWN BOOKS FOR YOUNG READERS
www.lbkids.co.uk

LITTLE, BROWN BOOKS FOR YOUNG READERS

First published in Great Britain in 2013 by
Little, Brown Books for Young Readers
Reprinted 2013

Copyright © 2013 by Lamps On Productions

The moral right of the author has been asserted.

A CIP catalogue record for this book
is available from the British Library.

ISBN 978-0-349-00159-3

Typeset in Cantarell by M Rules
Printed and bound in Great Britain by
Clays Ltd, St Ives plc

Papers used by LBYR are from well-managed forests
and other responsible sources.

 MIX
Paper from
responsible sources
FSC
www.fsc.org   FSC® C104740

Little, Brown Books for Young Readers
An imprint of
Little, Brown Book Group
100 Victoria Embankment
London EC4Y 0DY

An Hachette UK Company
www.hachette.co.uk

www.lbkids.co.uk

To my mum Pat,
who encouraged me to do my
homework in between kicking a ball
all around the house, and is still
with me every step of the way.

Welcome to a fantastic fantasy league – the greatest football competition ever held in this world or any other!

You'll need four on a team, so choose carefully. This is a lot more serious than a game in the park. You'll never know who your next opponents will be, or where you'll face them.

So lace up your boots, players, and good luck! The whistle's about to blow!

The Ref

CHAPTER 1

At the edge of the pitch, Max
strained at his lead, barking madly.
Frankie knew how he felt. This
game was *really* close. St Peter's
School had a good team. Maybe
even as good as Frankie's. The
score remained nil–nil, so the
pressure was building. Loads

of parents, Frankie's included, had turned out to watch the game.

"Concentrate, team!" called Mr Donald, their football coach. "Two minutes to go! Play to the final whistle."

Charlie had the ball in his gloves in the centre of the goal, looking for someone to throw it to. He saw Frankie's friend Kobe and rolled it out to him.

"Pass it, Kobe!" called Louise.

Kobe neatly sidestepped with the ball as one of the St Peter's team ran towards him. He kicked a looping pass to Louise. She managed to cushion the ball on her knee.

"Great!" said a voice from the side of the pitch. "Pass it to a *girl.*"

Frankie shot a frown at his brother Kevin, who was holding Max's lead. "She's better than you, any day of the week," he shouted back.

Kevin pulled a face. "Whatever."

"To me, Lou!" yelled Frankie.

Louise looked up. Two opponents rushed at her. She stabbed the ball with her toe, and it sailed perfectly between them to Frankie's feet.

"Go on, son!" shouted his dad.

Frankie turned and ran towards

the goal. It was just him and the keeper, a giant kid who'd stopped every shot so far.

"Shoot, Frankie!" yelled Louise.

The keeper started moving out from the goal, spreading his arms wide.

"You can do it!" called Frankie's mum.

Frankie wondered what to do. Dribble the ball around the keeper, or try for the chip over his head? The boy seemed taller by the second. He'd have to go around him. No problem. Frankie stepped over the ball, and dropped his shoulder to go left. The keeper kept

his eyes on the ball. Frankie darted right. He was through . . .

Argh!

He felt his legs snag as the keeper stuck out a boot and tackled him. He fell headlong on to the ground.

The crowd let out a groan.

Frankie sat up, a bit dizzy. The St Peter's goalkeeper had the ball in his hands.

"Bad luck," he said with a grin, then hurled the ball forwards.

"Get up, Frankie!" yelled Mr Donald.

Frankie scrambled to his feet and ran after it, but he was too far back.

It felt like he was watching in slow motion. The opposition passed the ball expertly between themselves, avoiding both Louise and Kobe and Matt. Their striker blasted the ball past Charlie and it nestled in the back of the goal.

The St Peter's players piled on top of each other as the whistle blew.

One-nil.

Frankie's team had lost!

They shook hands with the St Peter's kids. Frankie couldn't look Louise in the eye.

"I don't know what happened,"

he said, feeling his face grow hot. "I fluffed it."

His friend patted him on the back. "Don't worry," she said. "We can't win every game."

As the teams traipsed off the field, Frankie's brother blocked his path. "All right, bottler," he said.

"Leave him alone," said Charlie.

"Even *she* could have scored that," said Kevin, nodding at Louise.

"Is everything OK here?" asked Mr Donald, glaring at Kevin.

"Just giving a bit of encouragement, sir," sneered Kevin. Frankie's brother stalked off, tugging a whining Max with him.

Frankie sat on the grass and took off his boots. As he dropped them into his kitbag, his battered football rolled out.

"Oh dear," said Mr Donald. "If you've been practising with that old thing, it's no surprise you've been struggling."

Frankie shared a glance with Charlie and Louise. True, the ball did look like it had been chewed up and spat out again, but only Frankie and his friends knew the ball's appearance was deceiving. The football was magic – a gateway to other worlds. He couldn't help the flicker of a smile on his lips.

"I don't think it's funny," said Mr Donald. "You shouldn't try so many tricks, Frankie. Just get the basics right."

"Sorry, sir, it's just . . . " Frankie began.

But Mr Donald had walked away.

After they'd changed, Frankie's dad came over with Max. "You want a ride home, Frankie?" he asked. "We have to go via the shops to get Kevin some new clothes."

Frankie shook his head. He couldn't think of anything worse than sharing the back seat with his older brother taunting him. "It's OK, Dad," he said. "I'll walk Max back.

We'll go the long way, through the fields."

"We'll come with you," said Louse.

"Yeah, we can get some sweets on the way!" said Charlie.

They didn't talk about the game on the way home, which suited Frankie fine. It wasn't like him to lose his nerve at all. He kept replaying the chance in his head, wondering what he could have done differently.

Their route back to town took them past Evans' Farm.

"I'll show you the horses," said Louise.

Louise mucked out the stables
at the farm every weekend, and in
return was allowed to ride some of
the horses. The farmer, Mr Evans,
was fixing a fence post near the
road.

"Hello, Lou!" he said, waving a
mallet.

"Hi, Mr Evans," said Louise. "Do
you mind if I take my friends to see
Tinkerbelle?"

"Go right ahead," said the farmer.

"*Tinkerbelle?*" said Charlie, as
they crossed the yard. "What a silly
name for a horse!"

Louise led them into a barn,
past rows of empty stalls. As they

reached the last stall, Louise said,
"Meet Tinkerbelle."

Charlie gasped and took a step
back as a huge black head peered
over the door. "He's massive!" he
said.

Louise grinned. "He's a she,

15

actually. Sixteen and a half hands tall. Big softy, though, aren't you?" she said, stroking the horse's nose.

Max gave a little bark, and Tinkerbelle tossed her mane.

"Do you want to say hello, Frankie?" Louise asked.

Frankie let the football roll out of his bag. "I'm OK," he said glumly. He practised a couple of step-overs. Maybe Mr Donald was right. He'd tried to be too clever.

Charlie slowly approached Tinkerbelle, his gloved hand outstretched.

"Why don't you take those off?" said Louise. "She won't bite."

Charlie chuckled. "No way. You know me – always ready."

Frankie managed a smile. He spotted a horseshoe hanging on the wall opposite the stall by a nail. They were supposed to be good luck, weren't they?

Maybe if I can hit the horseshoe with the ball, I'll get lucky in front of goal next time, he thought.

He took aim, then gently chipped the ball. It sailed in a perfect arc towards the horseshoe . . .

. . . and vanished.

"Er . . . guys," he said, turning towards his friends.

Tinkerbelle gave a panicked

snort and Louise and Charlie spun around.

"Uh oh," said Charlie.

"Cool!" said Louise.

Max yelped.

The horseshoe and the stable wall had gone, replaced with a swirl of colour.

"Ready for another adventure?" asked Frankie.

CHAPTER 2

Frankie led the way, closing his
eyes as he passed through the
wall. When he opened them, the
farm had gone. He found himself
standing at the end of a dusty
street lined with ramshackle
wooden buildings. One was painted
above the door with a sign saying

"General Store". Another looked like a tavern, with a wooden veranda and swing doors. Shutters covered most of the windows. Beyond the street stretched miles of sandy desert dotted with cacti, and in the distance mountains rose in a haze of heat. What looked like a single line of rail track vanished into the distance. The magic football was resting alongside a water trough outside a blacksmith's stall.

Frankie sniffed – the air smelled strangely sweet, like caramel.

"Where *are* we?" asked Charlie. Instead of his school uniform, he was now wearing faded jeans and shirt with a neckerchief and a wide-brimmed hat.

"*When* are we?" asked Louise, who was tugging at the hem of a frilled red dress. "This is not my style at all!"

Frankie glanced down at his own clothes. He saw boots with spurs, trousers with leather chaps and a brown shirt. Stitched into the shirt was his FFC logo.

We must be here to play a game!

Max scampered along, sniffing the ground. "Looks like the Wild West to me!" he barked.

"How do you know?" asked Frankie.

The little dog wagged his tail. "You know when your dad's asleep on the sofa on Sunday afternoons with the TV on?"

"Yes," said Frankie.

"Well, I watch the Westerns," said Max. "I love John Wayne. Plus, you're wearing a cowboy hat. It's obvious, really."

Frankie reached up and felt the hat on his head. "Oh yeah."

"Let's explore," said Louise.

As they walked slowly up the centre of the street, eerie silence settled over them. Gusts blew in

from time to time, scattering sand in the air.

"Where are all the people?" said Charlie, shielding his eyes from the glaring sun. "This place seems deserted."

Frankie thought he saw the shape of a face in a window, but it quickly vanished.

"They're hiding," he said. *I wonder why.*

But not everyone was indoors. A grand white building stood at the end of the street. Above the double doors, a man stood at the top of a ladder with a rag. He was polishing a large clock that said it was eleven o'clock.

As they approached, Frankie spied a sign hanging above the doors, which read "Express train coming through at twelve o'clock today!"

"Hello there!" said Frankie.

The man spun around, and the ladder wobbled beneath him. Frankie rushed forwards and grabbed it before it fell. The man wore a black suit, with a thin black tie. A whistle hung around his neck. Beneath his bushy white beard, his face looked sort of familiar.

"You're the Ref!" said Frankie.

The man took out a pair of spectacles from his top pocket and put them on. He squinted at Frankie and his friends.

"I don't know what you're talking about," he said. "I'm the station master here in Sweetsville."

"Sweetsville?" said Charlie. "Sounds like my sort of place!"

"We're Frankie's FC," said Louise.

The station master climbed down from his ladder, then pointed to the clock. "You're early then," he said.

"Early for what?" barked Max.

The station master didn't seem surprised that a dog was talking to him. He shambled inside the station building and came out clutching a newspaper. He opened

it up so Frankie could read the
front cover:

The Cowboy's Crew
vs
Frankie's FC
The Sweetsville Showdown
High Noon!

"High noon!" said Charlie. "Cool!"

"That's twelve o'clock to you,"
said Max.

Charlie scowled. "I know that,
fur-face."

Louise nudged Frankie. "I don't
like the sound of The Cowboy's
Crew," she said.

27

"No one does," said the station master. "The meanest group of bandits this side of the mountains, they are. Over in Candytown, they stole every bar of chocolate from the store. The kids there haven't seen sweets all summer!"

"That's awful!" said Charlie.

"And over by Jelly Mountain," said the station master, "they blew up the sugar mines! The folks up there have to make cakes with salt instead of sugar!"

"Yuck!" said Louise.

So that's why everyone's hiding, thought Frankie.

"No point standing around here,"

said the station master. "Why don't you go and rest in the tavern?" He nodded across the street. "No milkshakes, I'm afraid. Tex made sure of that. Just water."

"A rest sounds good," said Charlie, wafting his hat in front of his face. "It's hot out here!"

"A glass of water will be fine," said Frankie, "but then we have to practise."

He led his team back across the street, kicking the ball in front of him. The Cowboy's Crew would be tough opponents, no doubt. *We'll have to do some passing drills. Then shooting.* A bead of sweat trickled down his back. *We'd better not tire ourselves out though.*

Max ran ahead. "Let me go first, guys," he said. "In the movies, these taverns are a bit rough-and-tumble. They don't like strangers, so you need to speak the lingo to fit in."

He scampered beneath the swing doors, and Frankie pushed through after him. A bell rang above.

"Howdy, partners," Max said. "We're just passin' by . . . Oh."

Frankie laughed. The tavern wasn't what he was expecting at all. There were no tables, no drinkers, and no bar. In fact, it wasn't a tavern at all.

"Awesome!" said Charlie. "A sweet shop!"

But then his face fell, and Frankie saw why. Though hundreds of jars filled the shelves on the wall, nearly all were empty. Some had a few boiled sweets in the bottom, others contained one or two chocolates or toffees. Trays on the counter had a few dusty sugared jellies. Frankie saw a pot with a single lollipop, and some ancient-looking gobstoppers and marshmallows.

"Coming!" called a voice, then a plump woman with frizzy hair shuffled up behind the counter. "Greetings," she said. "What can I . . .?"

The shopkeeper tailed off and her face drained of colour. She was staring at Louise and her mouth opened and closed like a gasping fish.

"Oh my giddy gumdrops!" she cried. Then she bustled out into the street screaming, "Sheriff! Sheriff Quigley! Come quick!"

CHAPTER 3

"What's got into her?" asked
Louise.

Charlie opened a jar on the
counter and sniffed suspiciously.
"Who knows?" he said. "Maybe
she didn't like your dress
either!"

Frankie took the chocolate out

of Charlie's hand and placed it on the counter. "These aren't ours," he said. "Plus, we're playing in an hour. You don't want to be sick."

"She just walked in, plain as day!" came the shopkeeper's voice from outside. "Be careful, Sheriff. She's dangerous!"

The swing doors opened again, and a tall grey-haired man wearing a starred sheriff's badge strode into the sweet shop. He placed his hands on his hips, and Frankie saw he had a gun in his holster. The woman who owned the shop peered out from behind him, trembling.

"Listen here," he said. "We don't

want any trouble, miss. You're coming with me to jail."

"Jail?" said Louise. "But I haven't done anything wrong."

"Don't make this hard," said the sheriff, stepping forwards.

Charlie stood in his path, shielding Louise with his gloves. "You leave her alone!" he said.

Quick as a flash, the sheriff drew his six-shooter and fired at Charlie's feet. Max leapt into the air and Frankie froze.

When the smoke from the barrel cleared, Frankie saw something white smeared just in front of Charlie's toes. Max sniffed at it.

"Chewing gum," he growled.

"Urgh!" said Louise. "That's gross!"

"The next time you won't be so lucky," said the sheriff. "Out of the way, kid."

Charlie stood his ground, but Louise touched him on the shoulder. "It's all right," she said. "I'll go with him and get this sorted out."

The sheriff tied Louise's hands with what looked like a strawberry lace and led her out of the shop. Frankie followed with Charlie and Max. The station clock read twenty past eleven. *We can't*

afford for Lou to be locked up,
he thought. *The game's in forty*
minutes and we haven't got any
subs!

"This is a big mistake," Max said.

"It was a mistake trying to rob
my shop!" cried the shopkeeper.
"I can't believe the legendary Miss
Sue-Ann just rode into town."

"Who's Miss Sue-Ann?" asked
Charlie.

The jailhouse was a stone
building across the street. Pinned
to the front wall were several
sheets of wind-blown paper, each
one showing a drawing of a face
with the word "WANTED" above.

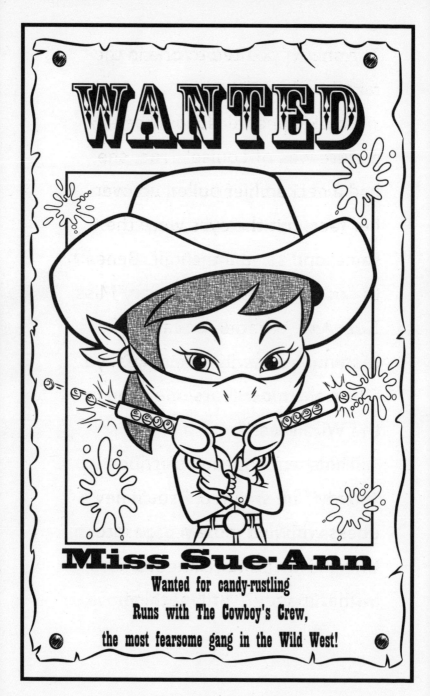

The sheriff pointed to one in the middle. "There she is!"

Frankie peered closer. The picture was of Louise! True, she had a neckerchief pulled up over her face, but the eyes were the same, and so was the hair. Beneath the portrait were the words: "Miss Sue-Ann. Wanted for candy-rustling. Runs with The Cowboy's Crew, the most fearsome gang in the Wild West!"

The sheriff opened the door. "Sandy!" he shouted. "You'll never guess who just moseyed on into town!" No answer came from inside. "Sandy?" Still nothing.

Sheriff Quigley growled. "That good fer nothing . . . " he said. "Late again."

He unfastened Louise's wrists, shoved her inside then started munching on the strawberry lace. He pointed a finger at Frankie's chest. "You and your sweet-toothed gang better lie low. Tex and the rest of his crew will be here soon, and you don't want to get in their way."

"But we're here to play them!" said Frankie.

"Then good luck to you," said the sheriff. "You'll sure need it!"

He turned and followed Louise

into the jailhouse, slamming the
door behind him.

Charlie slumped on to the step
and let his head fall into his gloves.
"What do we do now?" he said.

Frankie couldn't think of an
answer. This was bad. Really bad.

Max nudged him with his nose. "Come on, fellas," he said. "We can still win. It's just like Lou's been red-carded and sent off. We'll play on."

Frankie shook his head. "Lou's never even been given a *yellow* card before. She's the fairest player I know."

"Maybe we can break her out!" said Charlie, his face brightening. "Isn't that what they do in the movies, Max?"

Frankie's dog whined. "Normally they use dynamite. I'm guessing you haven't got any hanging around?"

Charlie buried his head again.

Frankie eyed the clock. Not long till the game. What if they lost? *If we don't win we might never get home* . . .

The sound of pounding hooves interrupted his thoughts. Across the street, they saw the sweet shop owner scurry indoors. More shutters banged closed.

In a cloud of dust, three horses galloped into town.

"It looks like The Cowboy's Crew is here," said Frankie.

CHAPTER 4

The lead horse was a brown stallion, ridden by a tall, lean man with a moustache, spinning a lasso over his head. He wore a tight-fitting suit with a black hat, and black boots. Thick stubble covered his cheeks and he chewed what looked like a piece of liquorice in blackened teeth. His nose had a kink in the middle where it had been broken.

"It must be Tex," Frankie whispered to the others.

A girl rode a smaller horse, with a scarf pulled up over her face. Frankie recognised her at once from the "Wanted" poster. Miss Sue-Ann. As her horse skidded to a halt, she tugged down the scarf and gave a nasty smile.

"She looks nothing like Louise!" said Charlie.

The final rider was a chubby man wearing clothes that were much too small. His shirt buttons were popping, and his belly hung over the top of his trousers. His hat was a huge, floppy-brimmed sombrero. He took it off and fanned his sweating pink face. His mouth had melted chocolate smeared around it.

"Looks like they've only got three players too," said Max.

"'Fraid not, fluffball," said Tex. "Spike, where are ya?"

Sand blew down the empty street, but no one came.

"Spike! Get out here now!" Tex called.

After another minute of waiting, a thin shadow fell on the street from between two buildings. Then out walked the strangest thing

Frankie had ever seen. It was a green cactus, six feet tall and covered in sharp spines. Its eyes were two holes at the top, with a dark slit for a mouth.

"Darn it, Tex," it said. "I was sunbathing out there."

"Meet Spike," said Tex with a grin. "The prickliest customer in the West."

"And the laziest," muttered Miss Sue-Ann.

The cactus waved a spiny arm at her, and she backed away on her horse. "Quiet, little lady," he said, "or you'll have more holes than a honeycomb."

Frankie stepped forwards and

dropped the ball to the ground.
"We're not scared of you," he said.
"Let's play."

At that very moment, a loud
hooting sound filled the air.
Everybody turned towards it. In the
distance, Frankie saw a cloud of
smoke spouting into the sky.

"Looks like the Express is early,"
said the fat man on Tex's team.

Tex's eyes narrowed and glinted.
"Change of plan then," he said. "We
won't be playing football today,
team."

"Aw, why not?" said Spike the
cactus. "I was looking forward to
beating these critters."

"Because we got a train to rob!" said Tex.

Frankie shot Charlie a glance. "This isn't right," he said.

"It's none of our business," said Charlie.

"We can't let them rob the train," said Max. "A real cowboy would stop them."

"You're not a real cowboy," said Charlie. "You're just a . . . "

Frankie left them arguing and rushed to the door of the sheriff's office. He banged on it with his fist until the sheriff opened up. The old man's face looked angry. "I told you before, unless you want to join your friend here . . . "

"Sheriff, The Cowboy's Crew is here and they're going to rob the Express train," said Frankie.

The sheriff's eyes widened, then he pushed past Frankie and shuffled out into the street, drawing his gun.

"Hold it right there, Tex," he shouted. "You're going to jail!"

A lasso fell over the sheriff's shoulders. Tex laughed and gave it a tug, pulling him off his feet. Sheriff Quigley struggled, but the ropes were too tight. "Why, you varmint!" he cursed. "Let me out this instant. When Deputy Sandy gets into town, you'll pay for this."

"Oh, is that right?" said Tex. "What do you say, Sandy?"

The fat man rode up on his horse. "Sorry, Sheriff," he said, stuffing another chocolate bar into his mouth. "I'm with Tex now."

The sheriff goggled. "Sandy, but you're a *sworn* deputy!"

Sandy pulled something out of his pocket and threw it to the ground, along with the chocolate wrapper. Frankie saw it was a law badge. "Not any more," he said. "Being an outlaw's much more fun."

Frankie ran forwards and started to loosen the ropes around the sheriff, and Max joined him. He heard a click and turned to see Tex pointing the barrel of a pistol right at him. "Enough," said the villain. "This thing's loaded with chewing gum. All of you are going to spend some time behind bars.

Max growled as Miss Sue-Ann took the sheriff's gun and pointed it at him. "Don't fight," said Frankie. "Remember how long it takes to get chewing gum out of your fur."

"Inside," said Tex, nodding to the jailhouse. Spike approached menacingly. Frankie didn't fancy getting anywhere near those spines. "Come on, guys," he said. "We don't have a choice."

All three of them were pushed into the jailhouse with the sheriff.

Louise saw them from her cell. She ran to the bars. "What's going on?" she said.

"We got you some company is what," said Sandy.

He unlocked the cage and shoved Frankie, his friends and the sheriff inside. The door clanged shut again. Sandy hung the keys on a peg on the opposite wall. "Someone might come for you in a few days," he said. "See ya, Sheriff."

He walked out, chuckling to himself.

"What now?" asked Charlie.

Frankie grabbed the bars and tried to bend them. He strained until he thought his bones would break, but they didn't budge. Charlie tried too, and Louise. They all fell back panting.

"You're wasting your time," sighed the sheriff, shaking free Tex's rope from his shoulders.

"They're solid iron. Better just relax and wait this one out." He sat on the floor and tugged his hat over his eyes.

"We need to beat Tex," said Louise. "Otherwise we're stuck here."

"Maybe Max can squeeze through the bars," said Charlie.

The little dog cocked his head. "It'll be a tight squeeze."

"Just try," said Charlie.

Max pushed his head between the bars, and wriggled. He got about halfway, but no further. "It's too narrow," he whined, scrambling loose and back into the cell.

"Too many doggy treats, you mean," said Charlie.

The group fell silent. "What's on that train, anyway?" asked Frankie.

The sheriff spoke from beneath his hat. "The biggest shipment of sweets you've ever seen," he said. "If Tex steals them, the kids in all the towns around won't have sweets for a year."

"Nightmare!" said Charlie.

Frankie stared at the keys hanging on the peg. *There's got to be some way of reaching them*. He kicked the football against the wall in frustration. As it bounced back, an idea hit him.

"Guys," he said. "I think I might have a plan. Give me your shoelaces."

"How's that gonna help?" asked Sheriff Quigley.

"Just do it," said Louise. Soon Frankie had four laces, all a couple of feet long. He tied them together and wrapped one end around the old football.

"I get it!" said Louise.

"I don't," said Max.

Frankie pushed the ball between the bars. It was just deflated enough to fit. Then, holding one end of the laces in his left hand, he threw the football towards the peg. It bounced off the wall right next to them.

"Oh, clever!" said Charlie. "Try again."

On the second attempt, Frankie knocked the keys off the peg and they clattered to the floor. He threw the ball again and it landed on top of them. Tugging the laces, the ball dragged the keys towards him. In no time at all, he had them in his hands.

"Good thinking, kid," said the sheriff.

Frankie turned the keys in the lock and the door *thunked* open. He turned to the others with a grim smile. "Time to stop The Cowboy's Crew," he said.

CHAPTER 5

They peered out from the jailhouse.
The street was quiet. Tex had tied
his gang's horses to a hitching post
in front of the station house. The
train was pulled up behind. "This is
mad," said the sheriff. "They've got
weapons! I bet chewing gum bullets
really bruise!"

"We've got this," said Frankie, holding up the sagging magic football.

"And this," said Louise, retrieving the lasso rope from the cell.

"And these," said Charlie, waving his goalie gloves.

Everyone looked at Max. "I've got my cowboy know-how," he said. "And sharp teeth."

"You don't have to come," said Frankie to the sheriff. "This is our problem."

Sheriff Quigley grinned. "Good idea. I'll hold the fort here."

Frankie rolled his eyes and walked out. They crept across the dusty street silently and walked up alongside the station house. Frankie paused at the corner of the building and edged his head around. The station master was standing with his arms above his head, Tex's gun pointed at his chest, while Sandy unloaded crates from a carriage. Spike was basking in the sun with his arms out.

"Hey, porcupine!" said Tex. "Don't go setting down roots there. Help Sandy."

Grumbling, Spike shuffled over and stabbed a crate with his arms, hoisting it off the train.

Soon they had a dozen crates on the platform.

"Check them," said Tex.

Sandy took a crowbar and inserted it under one of the crate's lids. He levered it off with a crack, and a grin spread over his face.

"It's gold, boss!" he said. "Pure gold."

He lifted a gold nugget the size of an egg out of the crate and held it up to the light. Frankie frowned. *I thought it was sweets they were after.*

"Let me see," said Miss Sue-Ann.

Sandy tossed the nugget to her, and she unwrapped it. She threw the gold wrapper on the platform, and bit into what was inside.

"It's chocolate!" whispered Charlie over Frankie's shoulder.

"Stop drooling," said Max.

"Right," said Frankie. "We need to work as a team. If we all rush at them together, they won't have time to draw their guns."

"Like a defence with too many forwards to mark," said Louise.

"I'll handle Tex," said Frankie. "Ready?"

Charlie nodded. "I'm always ready."

"Sure thing, partner," growled Max.

Frankie put his fingers to his lips and let out a whistle. All of Tex's gang looked up. Frankie dropped the ball and volleyed it at Tex. It struck his hand and sent the gun spinning into the air. Charlie ran forwards, dived, and caught it. Miss Sue-Ann went for her gun, but the lasso dropped over her shoulders, pinning her arms.

Sandy was too quick. He leapt over a crate as Max dashed at him, and whipped his pistol out of its holster. He cowered behind Spike. "No one move!" he said, aiming it at Frankie. "This is loaded with gobstoppers and they sure hurt."

Charlie had his gun levelled at Tex. Miss Sue-Ann squirmed in the rope.

Tex smiled, showing off his blackened teeth. "Looks like we've got ourselves a stand-off," he said.

"It's almost noon," said Frankie. "How about we settle this the old-fashioned way – a game of football?"

Tex stared hard at Frankie, and Frankie held his gaze.

Then the cowboy nodded. "Sure thing. Put the gun down, Sandy.

We're going to school these children some hard lessons."

The two teams lined up at opposite ends of the street. The town had come alive at last. Shutters and door were flung open as the people of Sweetsville emerged from hiding. Frankie heard two old women muttering to each other under a parasol: "Three young 'uns and a dog. They aint got a chocolate's chance under a blazing sun!"

"And why's that boy wearing gloves? It must be eighty degrees in the shade."

Charlie must have heard. "The best keepers are always . . . oh, never mind." He brushed a lock of damp hair off his head.

Frankie let himself smile. Charlie would need to be *extra* ready if they were going to win today.

The teams had moved two wagons to act as goals. Charlie stood in front of theirs, and Spike the cactus was opposite, flexing his long green limbs. His spines glistened in the sunlight, deadly sharp.

The station master stood in the centre with the ball. "We play until the clock strikes twelve," he said. "The winner can take the train out of town, the losers are going to jail for a long, long time."

The crowd stopped chattering and silence fell over the street. Frankie eyed the clock: eleven fifty-seven. Only three minutes to go. He looked across at Louise. She wore a determined face. And Max stood ready to pounce. *We can do it*, thought Frankie.

The station master blew a whistle and Frankie ran for the ball. He got there before Tex, and avoided a sliding tackle. Deputy Sandy tried to barge into him, but Frankie managed to skip past and stay on his feet.

"Pass it!" he heard Louise
shout, but when Frankie looked
he saw Miss Sue-Ann was
marking her closely. Frankie
sprinted towards the goal. Spike
watched him with beady eyes,
spreading his limbs wide. *This is
my chance*, thought Frankie. He

aimed at the bottom corner and fired.

Spike shot out a leg, and the ball hit one of his spines. It stuck fast, rather than bouncing off. Frankie kicked the dirt in disgust.

Spike shook his leg, but couldn't get the ball off.

"Hurry up!" said Tex.

Spike managed to knock the ball from his leg, but it stuck to his arm instead. "Just a minute!" he muttered, thrashing his limb.

Max chuckled.

"Ball-hogger!" muttered Miss Sue-Ann.

The cactus keeper finally managed

to hurl the ball out to Sandy, already red-faced from running about. Frankie couldn't see Tex anywhere. Max scampered up to tackle the deputy, but as he got close a horse came charging on to the pitch. A quick glance and Frankie saw why — Tex was by the hitching post. *He must have untied it!*

The horse stampeded in front of Max, who just avoided being trampled. It gave Sandy time to pass the ball to Miss Sue-Ann. Quick as a whirlwind, she spun away from Louise and angled a shot at goal. She kicked up a load of dust too. Charlie had to cover his eyes to protect them, and the ball sailed into the back of the open wagon.

Tex punched the air. "That's more like it!" He looked down his broken nose at Frankie. "You won't be getting any candy in jail, scamp. One-nil to the Crew!"

CHAPTER 6

Charlie fished the ball out of the back of the wagon, looking glum. Frankie eyed the clock. Just over one minute left.

"Keep your heads up, team," said Frankie. "You know what Mr Donald says: 'Play until the final whistle.'"

Charlie rolled the ball out to Frankie. He saw Sandy barrelling towards him, sweat pouring from under his hat. His gait was so wide from riding horses, Frankie had no problem toeing the ball between his legs. Sandy tried to stop himself but it was too late. He tripped over the edge of a horse trough, and fell head-first into the water with a splash.

"He needed a bath," said one of the spectators.

"You idiot!" yelled Tex.

Frankie slid a pass along the ground to Louise. As soon as she had the ball, Miss Sue-Ann rocketed towards her. She was one of the quickest players Frankie had ever seen. Louise glanced up. Max scampered along the wing, but Tex was blocking the pass.

She's got no options! thought Frankie.

Then he saw one.

"Look up, Lou!" he cried.

Louise glanced upwards. Frankie knew how quickly her brain worked on the pitch.

She stabbed the ball high into the air with her left foot, away from everyone. The spectators groaned as well, thinking she'd mishit it. But the ball crashed right into the

"General Store" sign over the shop and bounced back on to the pitch. Right by Max's paws.

"Great pass, Lou!" shouted Charlie.

I knew she could do it! thought Frankie.

Max kept the ball close to his feet as he ran towards the goal. Tex charged up behind him, and Spike edged forwards, swinging his deadly arms. Frankie chanced a look at the clock. The hands were nearly vertical. Seconds until noon.

"Shoot, Max!" he said.

Max's paws were a blur of step-overs and dummies, his tongue lolling. Tex was almost on him. Spike narrowed the angles ahead.

"Shoot now!" cried Louise.

Frankie could hardly watch. The ball bobbled in front of Max, and the little dog thrust his head on to it. Spike wasn't ready for a header and flailed with his arm. The ball sailed over the top, and landed with a thump in the wagon's mouth.

Max rolled sideways and Tex tried to skid to a halt. But his momentum was too fast. He crashed into Spike and they fell over together.

"Ouch!" Tex cried. "Ooh! Get off me! Argh! Ouch!"

Frankie winced as he watched Tex jerk and writhe to free himself of the spines.

Louise was on her knees, tickling Max's stomach as he rolled over in celebration.

GONG! The clock struck noon.

"One–all!" shouted Charlie, clapping his gloves together.

Tex finally untangled himself, his suit torn to ribbons and red scratches covering his skin. He looked very angry indeed.

"There's only one way to decide the winner," he snapped, his eyes glinting as he pointed at Frankie. "A shoot-out between captains."

"No way," said Louise. "Frankie's not a gunslinger."

"Not my problem," said Tex. "We stand back to back, take ten paces, then turn and fire."

"You'd better be quick about it," said the station master. "The train goes any minute, and the next one's not for a month."

"I don't want to stay here a month," said Charlie. "There aren't any sweets!"

Frankie swallowed. "How about I use the ball instead of a gun?" he said.

Tex shrugged. "You can use a wet flannel if you like," he said, "but nothing travels as quick as a gum bullet."

"I'll do it," said Frankie.

Louise rushed up to him. "Frankie, don't," she said. "It's too dangerous."

"There's no other way," he said. "Just stand back, Lou."

He turned and stood with his back to Tex's, the ball at his feet. The station master hovered beside them. "I'll count to ten," he said. "You both ready?"

"I'm ready to show this upstart who's boss," said Tex.

"I'm ready," said Frankie. But already he was worried. If he kicked the ball at Tex, he might hurt him. And what was to stop a crook like that just shooting him anyway?

"Right . . . One!" began the station master. Frankie took a step, and a plan formed in his mind.

"Two . . . Three . . . Four . . . "

Frankie's heart was thumping. He tried to clear his head. He felt like he was back facing St Peter's, running towards the goal. *You know what you need to do,* he thought.

"Five . . . Six . . . Seven . . . "

Aim in your mind. See the target . . .

"Eight . . . Nine . . . "

Just focus . . . breathe in . . .

"Ten!"

Frankie spun round, and saw
Tex's hand reaching lightning fast
for his gun. He snapped his foot
round, almost by instinct, and
blasted the ball just as Tex levelled
his six-shooter.

The ball slammed into Tex's hand, and the cowboy's gun went off. Chewing gum whistled past Frankie's ear. Tex, arms flailing, staggered backwards, tripping over his own feet. He landed with a splat on his backside. The crowd gasped and Frankie realised why.

Tex was sitting in a pile of fresh horse manure. His nose wrinkled. "What? Urgh!" He tried to stand, but slipped over, covering himself more. The people of Sweetsville started to laugh.

"It's *not* funny!" said Tex, as he finally managed to stand. "Stop laughing!"

The spectators were doubled over, slapping each other on the back.

Tex's face blackened with rage. He looked to his gang. "Enough! I'm not losing to a bunch of kids! Seize them!"

But his gang didn't move.

"Spike, what are you waiting for?"

The cactus man shrugged his spiny shoulders. "They won fair and square, Tex."

"Sue-Ann, don't just stand there!" said Tex.

Miss Sue-Ann shook her head. "It's over, Tex."

"Call yourself an outlaw?" he said.

Miss Sue-Ann threw her gun to the ground. "Actually, I wouldn't mind just working for a living. Maybe I'll get a job in the sweet shop."

Tex stamped his foot with a squelch of manure. "Sandy, tie them up!"

But Sandy edged away. "I'm done, Tex," he said. He turned to Sheriff Quigley. "Would you have me back, boss? I'll work double shifts."

The sheriff thought for a long moment, then nodded. He pointed to Tex. "You can start by putting him behind bars."

The people of Sweetsville

broke into applause as Sandy and the sheriff gripped Tex by the shoulders.

He writhed but couldn't get loose. "Let go of me, you wretches!" The crowd parted as he was dragged towards the jailhouse. "You haven't heard the last of Tex!"

Frankie, laughing, felt a glove tapping him on the shoulder. It was Charlie and he didn't look happy.

"I think we'd better get going," said his friend.

Frankie peered over his shoulder. Sure enough, two jets of steam spouted from the train.

Slowly, it started to move.

CHAPTER 7

"Time to say goodbye!" yelled Frankie, snatching up his football. "Come on, guys!"

With Lou, Charlie and Max, he sprinted towards the train station building. The crowd cheered as they passed and the station master raised his hand to wave. "See you again soon," he said, with a twinkle in his eye.

Frankie burst on to the platform, and leapt over a crate of sweets. The train was picking up speed, tooting as it pulled out of the station. Frankie spotted a door and ran alongside. Louise got a foot on the step and hauled herself onboard. Frankie let Charlie go next. His thighs were pumping just to keep up.

"Wait for me!" barked Max. "I've only got short legs!"

Frankie saw Max darting along as fast as he could, but the train was quicker. Frankie hurled the ball to

Louise and bent down to scoop the dog up in his arms. He dashed after the train. But carrying Max slowed him down. *I can't keep this up for much longer . . .*

"Charlie! I'm going to have to throw Max to you!" he yelled.

"Eh?" said Max. "We didn't discuss this."

"You ready?" said Frankie.

"No!" said Max.

"I'm always ready!" said Charlie, holding out his gloves.

Frankie saw the end of the platform fast approaching. *I've not got long.* Taking aim, he hurled Max towards the door.

Charlie snatched him from the air and bundled him inside.

Frankie's legs burned and his heart pounded so hard he felt it might burst out of his chest. The train wheels chugged in a blur and smoke drifted from the engine.

I'm not going to make it . . .

"Come on, Frankie!" Louise shouted. "Don't give up."

Lou's words fired Frankie's spirit. He gritted his teeth and forced an extra burst of speed, throwing himself at the door. His fingers caught the edge and the train dragged him off his feet. Then he felt hands gripping his arms and yanking him onboard. He landed in a heap on top of Louise and Charlie.

"Thanks, guys," he said.

Once he found his feet again, he stuck his head out of the train door. Wind whistled past as the town of Sweetsville faded into the distance.

"Er . . . what now?" asked Louise. "Do you think this train will take us home?"

"Who cares?" said Charlie. "Look what I found." He prised the lid off a box and scooped out a handful of sweets. "Jelly beans!"

The train thundered on through the desert. Frankie scanned the horizon but couldn't see any sign of life or any landmarks. Then, ahead, he spied a tunnel, where the tracks plunged into a mountainside. He wondered what was on the other side.

"These are delicious!" said Charlie. "Do you guys want . . . "

The train reached the tunnel and darkness swallowed them. The carriage beneath Frankie's feet seemed to disappear. For a moment, he felt completely weightless, as if he was floating. Then he rolled over and over on the ground. He heard the others crying out. Max barked and several horses whinnied and snorted.

Frankie sat up and picked a piece of straw from his hair. Max was licking his face. As his eyes adjusted to the gloom, he realised where he was.

"The stables!" he gasped. "We're home."

Charlie shook the straw off his clothes and opened one glove. In it was a single bean.

"Sorry, guys, only one left," he said, and popped it into his mouth.

*

The following week, Frankie and his team were up against Ryle's Park School.

Louise ran down the wing past two players, then squared the ball sideways to Frankie. Just as he was about to shoot, a defender clipped his ankle and Frankie sprawled on the grass.

The Ref blew his whistle and pointed to the penalty spot.

Frankie picked himself up, grabbed the ball and placed it on the penalty spot. Mr Donald was standing behind the goal. "It's OK if you don't want to take it, Frankie," he said. "You know — after last week's miss? No one would blame you if you wanted Louise to have a go instead."

Frankie glanced at Louise. She smiled. "You take it, Frankie. We all believe in you."

Kevin was sulking on the sidelines with Frankie's parents. As Frankie took a few steps back, he heard his brother mutter, "The bottler returns."

Frankie let the words sink away, and focused on the ball. If he could beat Tex the outlaw in a shoot-out, scoring a penalty against Ryle's Park was nothing.

Just believe in yourself.

Frankie took three steps and swung his boot. It connected perfectly and drove the ball into the top of the goal. The net ballooned and Frankie's team cheered.

Frankie slid across the grass on his knees, lifted his hands to the sky, and shouted:

"YEE–HAW!"

ACKNOWLEDGEMENTS

Many thanks to everyone at Little, Brown Book Group; Neil Blair, Zoe King, Daniel Teweles and all at The Blair Partnership; Mike Jackson for bringing my characters to life; special thanks to Michael Ford for all his wisdom and patience; and to Steve Kutner for being a great friend and for all his help and guidance not just with this book but with everything.